First published in Belgium and Holland by Clavis Uitgeverij, Hasselt – Amsterdam, 2015
Copyright © 2015, Clavis Uitgeverij

English translation from the Dutch by Clavis Publishing Inc. New York
Copyright © 2016 for the English language edition: Clavis Publishing Inc. New York

Visit us on the web at www.clavisbooks.com

Cleo written and illustrated by Sassafras De Bruyn
Original title: *Cleo*
Translated from the Dutch by Clavis Publishing

ISBN 978-1-60537-263-1

This book was printed in March 2016 at Publikum d.o.o., Slavka Rodica 6, Belgrade, Serbia

First Edition
10 9 8 7 6 5 4 3 2 1

Cleo

Sassafras De Bruyn

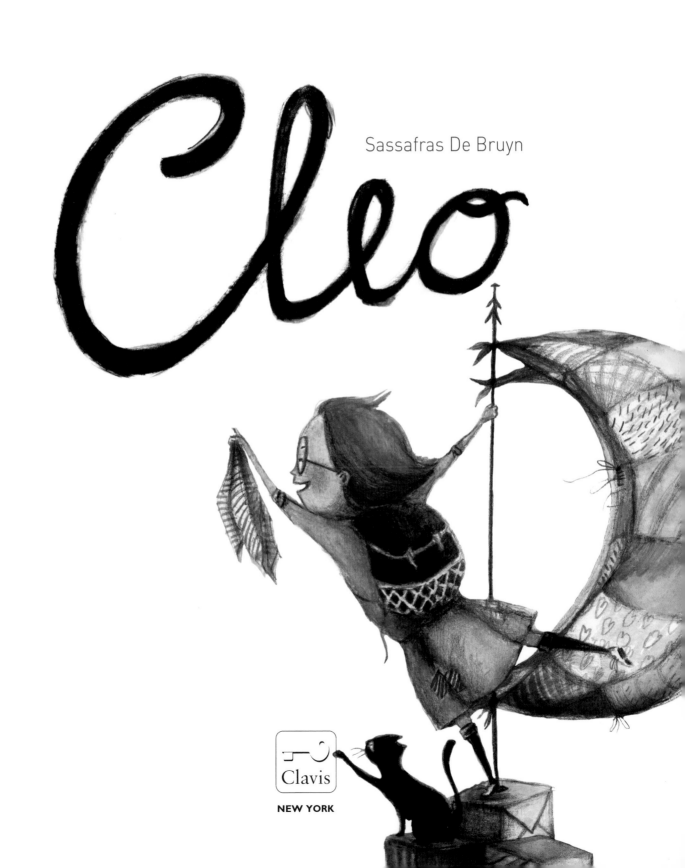

Clavis

NEW YORK

I always have to hurry.
I have to tie my shoelaces and comb my hair.
I have to count, write, run, play, go to the
bathroom, sleep, and above all listen.
Every day!

But one day I'll be out of here, wait and see.
I'll go to a place far away from here.
There'll be no more

"CLEO, QUICK, THE BUS IS WAITING!"
Or
"CLEO, TIDY YOUR ROOM!"

No more people who laugh at my glasses.

Yes, one day I'll pack my things. I will.
I won't let anyone come with me – except for Amadeus.
He's my brave black cat.
When he wants milk, he meows "MIIIILK!"
And when he wants to rip the wallpaper,
he doesn't ask, he just does it.
He is my VERY BEST friend.

I can already hear the wind
rustling in the sails.

"BYE-EEE! SEE YOU! FAREWELL!"

I sail away toward the horizon.

In a place
far away from here,
every day starts with a spectacular show.

I hold my breath
as the sky cities awaken.

At night I sail
through magic sea woods.
Suddenly a boy appears from
between the tree trunks.
"WHAT DO YOU HAVE THERE?"
he asks.

"STARS!" I say.
"I pick them from the trees
and keep them safe
because they bring me luck."

The boy sails with me to

THE MERMAID CAVES.

We dance and celebrate
until our feet hurt
and the sun rises again.

We defy FIERCE STORMS

and battle
HORRIBLE
SEA MONSTERS

Sometimes we tell stories
about giant frogs
and rivers of milk,
about waterfalls and the moon.

We are so good at telling stories
that the sea animals listen
with open mouths.

When we are tired
we climb into the clouds.

"JUST A LITTLE BIT HIGHER,"

says the boy, smiling.

Then we take a little nap in a heavenly bed.
The clouds are as soft as cotton wool,
and they taste like whipped cream.

We dance in the sun for hours
and sing all of our favorite songs.

TOGETHER
we can take on
THE WHOLE
WORLD!